Five reasons why we think you'll love this book!

Winnie AND Wilbur
IN WINTER

It snows in the middle of summer!

You can spot Santa ing past Winnie's h e.

The story is full of surprises.

There is so much to spot in every picture.

You can take the Winnie and Wilbur challenge: how many snowmen can you count?

Freya

Anushka

Maggie

Bailey

Johannes

Molly

Ashley

Amber

Jun-Yeong

Pablo

Matilda

Marwin

Hasan

Rebecca

Thank you to all these schools for helping with the endpapers:

St Barnabas Primary School, Oxford; St Ebbe's Primary School, Oxford; Marcham Primary School, Abingdon; St Michael's C.E. Aided Primary School, Oxford; St Bede's RC Primary School, Jarrow; The Western Academy, Beijing, China; John King School, Pinxton; Neston Primary School, Neston; Star of the Sea RC Primary School, Whitley Bay; José Jorge Letria Primary School, Cascais, Portugal; Dunmore Primary School, Abingdon; Özel Bahçeşehir İlköğretim Okulu, Istanbul, Turkey; the International School of Amsterdam, the Netherlands; Princethorpe Infant School, Birmingham.

For my wife Suzie—K.P.

OXFORD
UNIVERSITY PRESS

Great Clarendon Street, Oxford OX2 6DP

Oxford University Press is a department of the University of Oxford. It furthers the University's objective of excellence in research, scholarship, and education by publishing worldwide. Oxford is a registered trade mark of Oxford University Press in the UK and in certain other countries

British Library Cataloguing in Publication Data available

ISBN: 978-0-19-274830-0 (paperback)
ISBN: 978-019-274911-6 (paperback and CD)

10 9 8 7 6 5 4 3 2 1

Printed in China

Paper used in the production of this book is a natural, recyclable product made from wood grown in sustainable forests. The manufacturing process conforms to the environmental regulations of the country of origin

www.winnieandwilbur.com

VALERIE THOMAS AND KORKY PAUL

Winnie and Wilbur

IN WINTER

OXFORD
UNIVERSITY PRESS

Winnie the Witch looked out of her
window and shivered.
Her garden was covered in snow.
Her pond was covered in ice.
Icicles hung from the roof tops.
'I'm tired of winter,' said Winnie.

Wilbur came in through the cat flap.
His feet were wet, and his whiskers
were frozen.
Wilbur was tired of winter, too.

Suddenly, Winnie
had an idea.

She stopped what she was
doing, took down her Big Book
of Spells, and read it carefully.

Then she put on her woolly coat, her fluffy hat,
her snow boots, her gloves, and her scarf.
She picked up her wand and she went outside.

Wilbur already had a fur coat on, so he went
outside too. He thought something exciting
might happen, and he wanted to watch.

Winnie shut her eyes.
Then she stood on tiptoe, counted
to ten, waved her wand five
times, and shouted,

'Abracadabra!'

And something magical happened!

Above Winnie's house the sun shone brightly.
The sky was deep blue.
All the snow had disappeared.
It was no longer winter at Winnie's house.
It was sunny summer.

Winnie took off her woolly coat, her fluffy
hat, her snow boots, her gloves, and her scarf.
She got her deckchair and went out in the
garden to sit in the sun.
'This is lovely,' said Winnie.
'Summer is much nicer.'

Wilbur lay down in the sun and purred.
This is lovely, he thought.
Summer is much nicer than winter.

All over the garden, little
animals were waking up.
They had been having
their winter sleep, and
they were very cross.

They came out into the garden,
yawning sleepily. 'It's too early
for summer,' they grumbled.
'We want to go back to sleep.'

The flowers had been asleep
under the snow. They woke
up and began to grow.
Up came the leaves,
and then the flowers.

But the sun was too hot
for them. Their heads began
to droop. All the lovely
flowers were dying.

Winnie was worried.
The animals and the flowers
didn't like her lovely summer.

Then she heard a very
strange noise . . .

Winnie turned around, and there behind her
was a great crowd of people. They were
running along the road towards her house.

They crowded into her garden.
They took off their coats, their
hats, their boots, their gloves,
and their scarves.

They sat in the sunshine.
They walked on Winnie's flowers.
They put orange peel on Winnie's
grass. They paddled in Winnie's pond.

Soon there was no room for Winnie
and Wilbur in the garden. They went
inside and looked out of the window.
The noise was horrible.
The mess was horrible.
Winnie's lovely summer was horrible.

Then Winnie heard another strange noise.

A tinkling noise . . .

Somebody was selling ice creams in her garden.

Winnie was furious.
She grabbed her wand.
She rushed outside.
She stamped her foot, shut her eyes, counted
to ten, waved her wand five times and shouted,

'Abracadabra!'

The sun disappeared.
The blue sky disappeared.
And the snow began to fall.

The people put on their coats, their hats, their boots,
their gloves, and their scarves, and rushed home.
The animals went back to bed, to finish their winter sleep.
The flowers went back under the ground to wait for spring.

Winnie and Wilbur went
back inside. Winnie made
a cup of hot chocolate and
toasted a muffin. Wilbur
had a saucer of warm milk.

Then Winnie snuggled into bed. Wilbur
curled up at the foot of the bed and purred.
'This is warm and cosy,' said Winnie.
'Winter is lovely too.'

Bethany

Katia

Eun-Jae

Kathleen

Ji-Eun

Jenny

Sara

Fraser

Ka Keung

Selin

Selin

Olivia

Siyabend

Kieran

A note for grown-ups

Oxford Owl is a FREE and easy-to-use website packed with support and advice about everything to do with reading.

Informative videos

Hints, tips and fun activities

Top tips from top writers for reading with your child

Help with choosing picture books

For this expert advice and much, much more about how children learn to read and how to keep them reading ...

LOOK
for Oxford Owl
www.oxfordowl.co.uk